An I Can Read Book®

Aunt Eater Loves a Mystery

by Doug Cushman

SCHOLASTIC INC.

New York   Toronto   London   Auckland   Sydney
Mexico City   New Delhi   Hong Kong   Buenos Aires

For Rebecca and Jan,
the Best

ISBN 0-590-10445-4

12 11 10 9 8 7 6 5 4   4 5 6/0

Printed in the U.S.A.   23

First Scholastic printing, November 1996

Contents

Aunt Eater Rides the Train

Aunt Eater the anteater
loved mysteries.
She took her mystery books
everywhere she went.

One day Aunt Eater decided

to visit her sister, Eliza.

She packed two dresses,

two mysteries,

a sweater, and five bags

of popcorn kernels.

"Eliza loves popcorn,"

said Aunt Eater.

Aunt Eater walked

to the train station.

People hurried this way and that.

"They all look like people

in my mystery stories,"

Aunt Eater thought happily.

A porter said, "Excuse me.

May I take your bag?"

"Yes," said Aunt Eater.

"I am in car five,

seat twenty-three."

Aunt Eater bought some candy

for the train ride.

Then she found her seat

and began to read a mystery.

The train rolled on and on.

Aunt Eater felt chilly.

She opened her bag

to get her sweater.

But the bag was filled

with hammers and screwdrivers

and all sorts of tools.

"This is not my bag!" she cried.

"My bag has been stolen.

Who would steal a suitcase

full of clothes and popcorn?

I must tell the conductor."

Aunt Eater found the conductor
and told him her story.
"We must find your bag,"
he said. "Come with me."

They talked to a banker,

a magician,

a doctor,

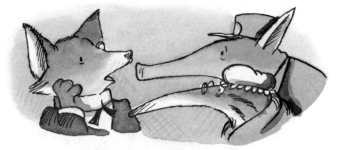

and a butler.

But no one had seen

the missing bag.

Suddenly they heard a loud *pop!*

Pop! Pop! Pop, pop, pop!

"It is coming from the engine!"

the conductor yelled.

Everyone ran to the front

of the train.

A black bag sat

beside the roaring boiler.

Popcorn was flying everywhere.

"That is my bag!" Aunt Eater cried.

18

"It looks just like mine,"

said the engineer.

"The porter must have switched

your bags by mistake,"

said the conductor.

"No harm done," said Aunt Eater.

"Let's enjoy the popcorn

while it is still hot."

And that is what they did.

Aunt Eater Sees a Shadow

Eliza was happy

to see Aunt Eater.

"I want you to meet

all my friends," she said.

"Tonight we will have a party."

That night

Eliza's house was filled

with her friends.

Alfred the butler

served little hot dogs on toothpicks.

He filled tall glasses

with lemon punch.

Aunt Eater told everyone

about her train ride.

"Exciting things never happen

in this town," Eliza said.

Suddenly,

Aunt Eater saw a dark shadow.

"Look!" she cried.

Everyone gasped.

Eliza's cat jumped

and knocked over the lamp.

The room went dark.

Aunt Eater found the light switch

and clicked on the light.

The black shadow was gone!

"Who could it have been?"

Eliza asked.

"It might be a jewel thief

looking for diamonds,"

said Aunt Eater.

"We must search the house."

Everyone ran to find the thief.

They looked behind chairs

and under beds.

No one found a thing.

Alfred served more punch.

"Yipe!" cried Eliza.

The shadow was on the wall again.

The cat fell into the punch bowl.

Alfred dropped his serving tray.

The shadow disappeared.

"Quick!" cried Aunt Eater.

"He may be outside!"

Everyone rushed outside.

They looked under trees

and bushes.

They looked behind the garage

and in trash cans.

But they found no one.

When everyone had gone home,

Alfred began to clean up.

"Who would think

that a mystery could happen here?"

he asked Aunt Eater.

Aunt Eater looked at Alfred.

Then she began to laugh.

"Look at your shadow," she said.

"This mystery has been solved."

Aunt Eater Collects Her Mail

Aunt Eater returned home.

She had lots of mail

in her mailbox.

There was a short note

on yellow paper.

"What is this?" she asked.

The note said:

I WILL BE BACK AT 3 O'CLOCK THIS AFTERNOON

"Part of the note is missing,"

said Aunt Eater.

"What does it mean?

Perhaps it is for Mr. Chumly

next door.

Sometimes he has strange people

in his house."

Aunt Eater began to wash

her windows.

She also watched

Mr. Chumly's house.

At three o'clock

a large, black car

drove up to Mr. Chumly's house.

A tall figure in a dark coat

got out of the car.

He had a scarf

around his neck.

He carried a large bag.

"Who would wear a scarf

in this hot weather?"

Aunt Eater asked.

"Maybe he is a thief.

He does not want people

to see who he is."

Aunt Eater grabbed the note

and a measuring cup.

"Well, *I* must find out!"

She ran across the yard

and knocked on Mr. Chumly's door.

Mr. Chumly opened the door.

"What a pleasant surprise,"
he said. "Please come in."

"I...ah...need a cup of flour,"
Aunt Eater stammered.

"Of course," said Mr. Chumly.

"But first meet my brother Lester.

He just brought back my laundry.

He runs a Laundromat."

"Nice to meet you," Lester whispered.

"You must excuse my voice.

I have a bad sore throat.

I need to wear this scarf

to keep my neck warm."

"Oh, dear," Aunt Eater thought.

She was very embarrassed.

Lester was not a thief.

"I am pleased to meet you,"

she said.

"Did you leave this note

for your brother

in my mailbox by mistake?"

"No," said Lester.

"This is a real mystery,"

said Aunt Eater.

Just then, the doorbell rang.

It was the mailman.

"Hello, Aunt Eater," he said.

"I thought I saw you come in here.

Did you get my note?"

"*You* wrote the note?"

Aunt Eater asked.

"Yes," said the mailman.

"I have a package for you."

"Thank you," said Aunt Eater.

"Solving mysteries makes me tired.

I think I will go home."

Aunt Eater went home

and opened her package.

Then she sat down in her cozy chair

and began to read

her latest mystery book.

Aunt Eater Solves a Mystery

Mr. Chumly knocked

on Aunt Eater's door.

"I am going to visit Lester,"

he said.

"Will you take care of Sam

while I am gone?"

"Of course," Aunt Eater said.

"I love cats."

"Thank you, Aunt Eater,"

said Mr. Chumly.

"Good-bye, Sam."

"You look hungry, Sam,"

said Aunt Eater.

"Here is some fish for you."

Sam sniffed the plate

and turned up his nose.

"Maybe you would like some milk,"

said Aunt Eater.

Sam lapped up the milk.

Suddenly the sky turned dark.

It began to rain.

Thunder roared

and lightning flashed.

All the lights went out.

"Oh, dear," Aunt Eater muttered.

"Where did I put the candles?"

She found some candles in a drawer
and lit them.

Sam was gone!

"Sam!" she called.

"Where are you, Sam?"

She looked under the sink

and behind the stove.

No Sam.

She looked upstairs and down.

Still no Sam.

"What will I tell Mr. Chumly?"

Aunt Eater asked.

Aunt Eater thought a minute.

"I should look for clues

like a real detective,"

she said.

She saw the open door.

"I bet Sam went outside."

The rain had stopped.

Aunt Eater saw a cat's paw prints

in the soft ground.

"A clue!" said Aunt Eater.

She followed the paw prints

down the street

and around the corner.

There the paw prints stopped.

"What would a detective do now?"

asked Aunt Eater.

She thought some more.

"Well," she said.

"Sam is an alley cat.

Maybe he went into that alley."

The alley was dark.

Aunt Eater's neck tingled.

"Maybe I should come back

tomorrow," she said.

Then she heard a meow.

"Sam!" she cried.

She rushed into the alley.

"Oh, my!" she gasped.

There were hundreds of cats.

They all looked like Sam!

"Sam!" she called. "Sam!

Which one of you is Sam?"

All the cats meowed.

"Oh, dear," she said crossly.

"How will I ever find Sam?"

Then Aunt Eater had an idea.

She ran down the street.

She came back with a package.

"Look, cats," she called.

"I have some nice fish for you."

Hundreds of cats

ran to Aunt Eater.

They all wanted the fish.

All except one cat.

Sam.

Aunt Eater carried Sam

back to her house.

She poured a bowl of milk for him.

She made a cup of cocoa

for herself.

"Let me read you

my new mystery,"

Aunt Eater said.

Aunt Eater sat down

and opened her book.

Sam drank his milk

and listened

late into the night.